The Glass Abattoir

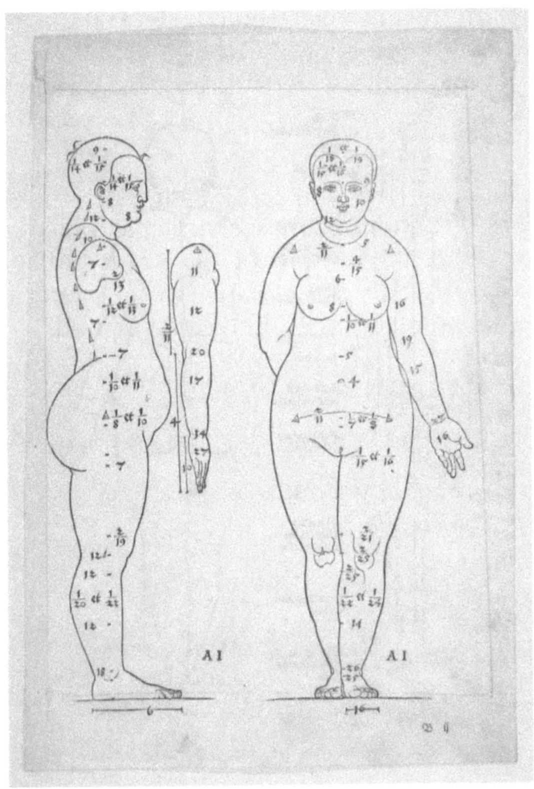

Matthew Kinlin

Cover design by Mike Corrao

Book design by Matthew Kinlin

www.dfllit.com

contact@dfllit.com

D.F.L.
LIT

I. CORPSE

II. WHORE

III. PHANTOM

IV. SLAVE

A tale of four women.

"When I was a child, I imagined the soul to be a dragon, a shadow floating in the air like blue smoke—a huge winged creature, half bird, half fish. But inside the dragon, everything was red."

— Ingmar Bergman

CORPSE

RED

RED

RED

A yellow flower clamped between the white knuckles of her small hands. Her fingers were always the smallest placed upon the keys of the piano, twisting and choking music from the broken instrument they had sent from Vienna. She liked to sit and listen to the Whore (red) play nocturnes as the moon fell sicker beneath their long dresses, the white swooping parasols they used to catch the summer sun and watch it drown in puddles at their feet like lovesick boys, blonde and blazing legs.

The Corpse (red) once gulped at blue air atop an Italian mountain and it was here, she questioned God Himself, her sick body swaddled and stitched with bags of lavender and cuckoo spit. Her mind was fed into the sanatorium clock and only then did she see the finiteness of her own small hands, how short each breath would fall across the open palms. A doctor came in a moleskin waistcoat and placed his silver heart to hers, asked her to shout into a vellum balloon—the black bladder of an Oberland cow. Alps teeming with air, cheese, milk: she dreamed of a cow as the gigantic mother of Switzerland, a river of warmth. She liked to walk amongst the fields at dusk and watch the cows, their kind and silent faces swallowed inside morning fog. She felt the strength of her mind begin to fail. She saw herself in a mirror in the drawing room. No longer human but some thin and silver shape like a lank piece of lace nailed to the door. When the Slave (red) came into her bed, she held the swollen breast to her cheek and they submerged inside the depths of another, green maps of varicose that ran along her shivering back as she played with the Slave's (red) locket ~~and the brown unfurling hair.~~

The Slave (red) was the only one, had placed a screen at the bottom of the bed of the Corpse (red) and showed her shadows: a master and a djinn; souls switched at midnight at the end of Merzouga, a gateway into Erg Chebbi—ocean of sand dunes. The Corpse (red) dreamed of vultures rising from valleys of jewels, their wings stretched out across the cold bare wall. She folded herself into the armpit of the Slave (red) and became a shadow herself, tied with rope and stretched across the wet bedsheets, her ankles and wrists cracking as the clocks continued to twist—churning, howling. The Corpse (red) was slow to rot. She was made to watch her skin turn white then yellow, purple patches of dead flesh appearing upon her immaculate stomach like wet fruit. She held the arm of the Phantom (red) and they staggered into the garden, down beyond the lake.

The swans folded their necks towards each other, curtseyed across the clear black waters. The pale sun was muted behind its final green leaves of summer rushing above their heads. The Phantom (red) spoke of a trip to the south and how well the Corpse (red) had seemed, the faith she had in Doctor Gustav. The Corpse (smiled) and kissed the Phantom (red) upon the cheek. She trusted only the swans and their greed. They braided their necks together into a ten-fold knot and each peered down into the black water for grubs and the silver fish that hid inside the mud. A feather-headed Medusa bobbing in the centre of the moonlit lake.

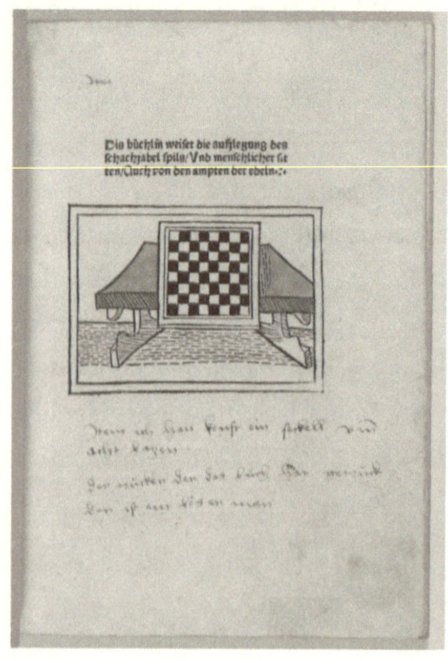

~~The Corpse (red) came away from the window. It was past midnight and the Whore (red) was asleep, held a book of romantic poetry, the musing of a baffled sodomite found dead in his Paris atelier. The Corpse (red) leaned down to read a few of the words beneath her sister's hand:~~ *O purple flower of Illyria! Hot and insane!* ~~She returned to bed and sank into the cancelled dreams of the dying, a sleep without rest: sleep only an extension of sorrow. She saw her candlelit sisters and the maid hung from their necks, the ruptured blood and faeces. She dreamed they each were quartered inside a machine with a single silver pincer. The pincer removed their clothing and tunnelled expertly beneath their skins to reveal wonderful and winding tumours, sixteen in total—a cancer in the shape of a blackberry.~~

The Corpse (red) came away from the window. It was past midnight and the Whore (red) was asleep, held a book of romantic poetry, the musings of a baffled sodomite found dead in his Paris atelier. The Corpse (red) leaned down to read a few of the words beneath her sister's hand: *O purple flower of Illyria! Hot and insane!* She returned to bed and sank into the cancelled dreams of the dying, a sleep without rest: sleep only an extension of sorrow. She saw her candlelit sisters and the maid hung from their necks, the ruptured blood and faeces. She dreamed they each were quartered inside a machine with a single silver pincer. The pincer removed their clothing and tunnelled expertly beneath their skins to reveal wonderful and winding tumours, sixteen in total—a cancer in the shape of a blackberry.

When she was young, she had been impregnated by a freiherr: a rich and decorated baron, blind and amber in one eye. The other was pale powder blue and searched her body harder due to working alone, scrambling up and down her arms and face as she removed the underskirt, her chocolate stockings. He was stacked high with war medals and Prussian blood, had ingested the forty souls of children he executed once in a field of rye and sugar beets. She had felt the sperm as cold as glass, and the blind eye remained very still so she kissed it closed. The Corpse (red) was filled with a child for three months before it fled into God's embrace. She did not even tell the Whore (red) who had peered at the freiherr from above the playing cards. The Corpse (red) was the Queen of Diamonds dressed in red earth, the sex of a fox now wet and open, treasured envy opening like a box of knives.

Norseman's Knock upon the table and the cards were flung into the air, the Whore (red) laughing and obnoxious. The Slave (red) smiled inside a dark corridor.

The freiherr showed them a trick, placing a wine goblet in the centre of the right palm of the Whore (red). He mumbled a few words in Bavarian, a curse exchanged by an old beggar for her life, as she wrapped herself in a loden cloth and ran into the forest. He told the Whore (red) to pull away her hand and she was shaking with tears of laughter, shining down her face. The most beautiful of them all, and gasped to see the goblet hovering in the air—nothing beneath, object floating like a ghost. The Corpse (red) remained completely still, watching the light shimmer on the cloth in eddies of strange rainbows as the Whore (red) laughed harder and harder, the impossible come true between them at the ordinary walnut table, throwing herself on the freiherr.

As night fell, she washed without the Slave (red) and heard the footsteps of the freiherr at the door. The Corpse (red) felt blessed, chosen over the Whore (red) and remained naked beside the enamel bowl and sponge, the water still glistening across her lower back and buttocks. His member was much darker than the flesh around, like a gnarled wand. And the Corpse (red) wondered afterwards for many years if maybe he *was* a magician, if with his Prussian curse, had placed his bad sperm inside her and now the worst wish had come true, her body beginning to break beneath a secret truce, the lies she told each day to her own sisters, her beating soul. And she felt no shame. Maybe the blood filling her lungs was the kissing of angels, the pink dust of Jupiter and Venus that circled her bed each night. She dreamed of the moon dipped in honey and falling into the lake at night. Her body was as pale as a swan risen from the bed, choking on its own breath, the rattling wings.

The Corpse (red) watched and calmly agreed to her own extinction. In the middle of the night, she heard footsteps once more in the hallway, the Slave (red) moving backwards into a solid wall to allow for the final visitor. It was Satan, dressed in midsummer silver, danced along the hallway in pools of mercury at his feet. Her face was white but he wiped strawberries across each eyelid. She was the beautiful daybreak of the dead, falling into sweeter and sweeter decay, carrion held to the breast of a stronger heart—always feeding, dappled in moonlit daffodils. Satan covered her in lilies, the sad looping necks of swans that bowed again in the fading light, the Phantom (red) weeping at the window at all the words that could never be said, the diaries she read for weeks afterwards. Satan handed the Corpse (red) a goose quill and his skeleton wrist held a white parchment. Heaven as a mirrored desert, a snow globe in the hands of the Slave (red) stood in the corner of the room.

The dead know everything, can see beyond the suffering of a child left in the marketplace, a machine built inside its expanding abattoir. She was now the extraordinary beyond as she wrote the words upon the page, fell through the desk into water everlasting, an island in a sea of hopeless ice. Surrounded the bed were skeletons dressed in green envy, diaphragms stapled with corsages of spruce branches. The soul of the Corpse (red) was a birch tree turned north-west into frost, the breath of Satan upon the windowpane—her body washed and span upside-down.

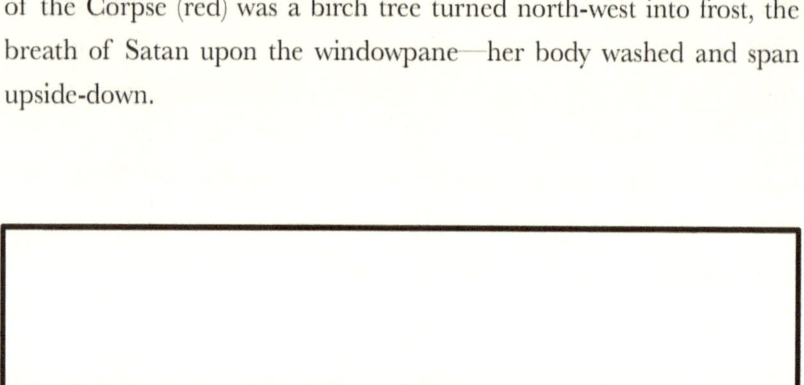

In the morning, before the sun had risen, the Phantom (red) and Slave (red) found the piece of parchment upon the writing desk. Blue-black ink scrawled upon the page. The dead can count to ten.

Meine Königin der Diamanten

I have seen your secret misery, shining like a silver thread through your head and laced up to the firmament, where in deepest Saturn I was called. The soul bleeds for its own exultation, to become the glory of each and every sin. I have watched every glance between the blood-soaked walls of my cage and the birds filled with songs of their daily torture and joy. I lay in a bathtub of lead with canaries in the platinum stream, your face revealed in the mouth of my cherished companion— Astaroth coiled upon his dragon that held a chalice filled with purest water. Across the surface, a vision cometh to me: two sisters atop an Italian mountain fell forwards onto a mountain in Jericho where the Christ-son Himself, in the dark shade of almond trees, knelt before my cloved feet. This secret filled your mind and I wished us to meet once more. Look upon the water's edge and see the Blå Jungfrun. Her face is quilted with blue veils and she wanders a labyrinth eaten by crows, Easter rushed across the first silver waves. To walk across water, turn stones into bread—are but simple acts of devilry. The transubstantiation of sperm into blood, the rings of Neptune dancing upon your smooth collarbone. Astaroth shall cometh on the third night, when your lungs scream for tulips, harebell, the backwards trinity drawn upon the floor before you. Three sisters reaching out into the red desert, a blue maiden washing your little feet. Every wish comes true in August, don't you see? The clocks are singing for now, my love. The secret shame of Christ, who knelt before Satan in the Jericho valley—is shared and glorious amongst the hearts of His children, glowing as they fill themselves with darkness. We gorge on the miserable freedom that escorts us to the marriage of the stars. Eighty moons tumbling from each eyelid. Why are you crying, my love? The sorrow is over, we begin always. All it takes is a kiss on the lips and Håkan the Red, every King of Sweden leaps from his grave. Sign me your eternal soul. We drink the sunsets and gallop into night. Hell is always tomorrow.

Yours, *Archduke Henrik von Buxhoevden*

25

RED

WHORE

RED

RED

Honeysuckle, sweetest at night, lost in her strawberry hair, loosened across the shoulders and then trampled beneath her large pink toe. The Whore (red) held a hand mirror close to her cheek so she might see how she looked to the wasps that followed her through the garden at noontime, pecking at lemon pastry the Slave (red) had left upon the kitchen sill. She watched the curious passion between each bee and its chosen flower as it locked itself inside, aligned its own shape with the symmetrical splatter on each petal: its strobing red shadow.

She took off a pearl earring, given by her grand-aunt that lay dead—whitened in arsenic and vodka, a virgin blasted into the chapel furnace.

She took off a pearl earring, given by her grand-aunt that lay dead whitened in arsenic and vodka, a virgin blasted into the chapel furnace. Laughing, she pierced the ovary of a smörboll flower. It smelt yellow and revolting, the opalescent jewel swaying like a pendulum, causing little turrets of pollen to twist upwards from the singing beast. Like the others, she was allergic to ivy and unknown weeds that grew in the dark blue shade. She remembered playing kurragömma with the Phantom (red) and seeing her face as she came out from beneath the bush covered in red and white hives, mouth bloated toad-like and unable to speak. She had placed eight-petal mountain-avens all along the windowsill of the Corpse (red) in the hope that an angel flying past might take pity upon her choking sister, carry her upon its back upwards a cold black staircase into the blue never, chimerical white waterfalls.

The Whore (red) dreamed of leaving on a train for China, of making love in a bed covered in red rooster and fireworks leaving her hands into the Americas. She had once bought a ticket to New York and gone at daybreak, stood alone at the harbour. She watched coal-caked hags wait in lines for a damp hammock aboard, fading like jellied amoebas beneath their potato-cloth shawls. A scared woman becomes a crawled version of herself. She had seen day break in the face of her own mother, a hysteric locked up in Malmö for plotting to murder her prodigious uncle, an earth scientist drunk in London. The Phantom (red) had gone to visit the Malmö asylum but she spoke of nothing, except once regarding the properties of helium, stared through the wall when asked a question or brushed her burning black hair.

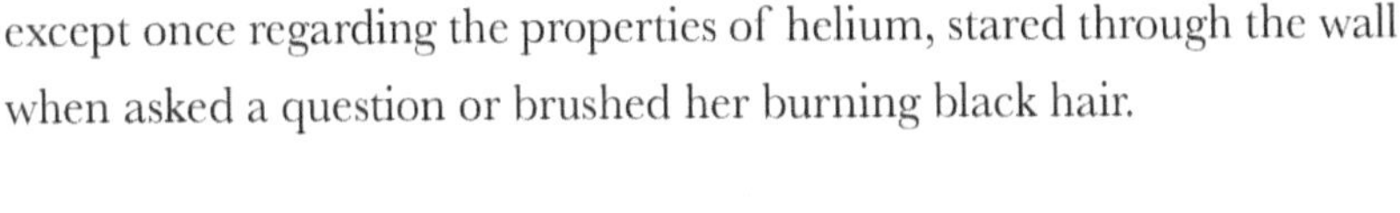

This was a house of silence now and flickering childhood games, a hopscotch scrawled across the broken back of the Corpse (red). She saw the garden in dazzled May, the lake like an ocean of the most glamorous fires. The grass was littered with wooden kubbar that they threw batons and balls at.

The Whore (red) pulled her hands away from her eyes to watch the Corpse (red) alive and maddened, take a mallet and hammer the king three feet into the ground. How the Whore (red) laughed! She laughed so hard that afternoon as they slept tickled in the bright green grass!

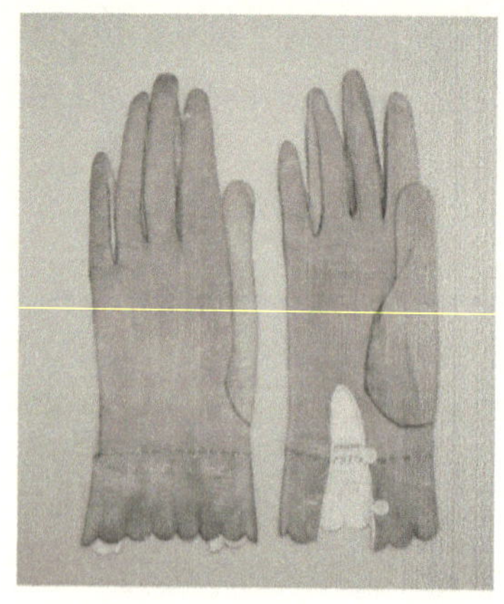

And when evening began to cool, she ran into the woodland beyond the lake to see her beloved, the farmer's son who cleaned the horses at dusk. She watched the setting orange and purple sky as he calmed the animals, stroked their long necks and backs sore from dragging the carts of wheat and rye between the fields and barn since dawn. When he turned to see her, she felt the foreboding of her own youth—her breasts already coming loose from the white corsage and unfolding in the hands of the shaking youth who rubbed the ends until she felt herself grow dizzy in the arms of the boy who stank of animal and manure, already unbuckling his trousers to pleasure her cunt, her mouth, her bespangled ass. She dreamed of America and wranglers with their pistols aimed at hurricanes of sand, their horses braying softly as they ran into blast.

The Whore (red), you see, wanted and deserved everything. She saw the body of the boy beneath her now, his face pink and afraid at the unspeakable, and she knew it to be hers. ~~She saw the bodies of the Corpse (red), the Phantom (red) and the Slave (red), and they were hers too.~~ The mansion itself was an abattoir that fed their lean bodies through the clocks chiming upon the mantelpiece, chewed and spat them out. When the farmer's son flew a cobweb of sperm across his face and chest, she tasted the ends of his fingertips and knew the boy's soul was her own, cowering with his back against the hollowed black tree. She left him in the grass like carrion, the ends of her white dress igniting with pride.

The Whore (red), you see, wanted and deserved everything. She saw the body of the boy beneath her now, his face pink and afraid at the unspeakable, and she knew it to be hers. ~~She saw the bodies of the Corpse (red), the Phantom (red) and the Slave (red), and they were hers too.~~ The mansion itself was an abattoir that fed their lean bodies through the clocks chiming upon the mantelpiece, chewed and spat them out. When the farmer's son flew a cobweb of sperm across his face and chest, she tasted the ends of his fingertips and knew the boy's soul was her own, cowering with his back against the hollowed black tree. She left him in the grass like carrion, the ends of her white dress igniting with pride.

When the Corpse (red) and the Phantom (red) left for Italy, she made
weekly trips to the city square and drank midwinter herbs in a bar filled
with harlequin wenches. A woman painted in a blue checkboard invited
her into a linen tent and asked to see her palm, said she could see an
earthly paradise—cascading pure waters, fish that made love in shoals
of hundreds, her hair washed in Indian milk. The Whore (red) laughed
and paid the blue woman with a silver brooch, Ethiopian butterflies
stolen and soaked in lead. On the morning the Corpse (red) passed
from the living into purple Valhalla, she had returned to bed and left the
Slave (red) to dress and wash her feet. The Slave (red) picked up each of
the eight-petal mountain-avens and let them fall naked like confetti
upon the cadaver. They formed a constellation and as night darkened,

insects came in through an open window to feed upon the sweetness of her decay.

At midnight all the clocks stopped, and the Whore (red), for the first time in her life, was afraid. She crept softly and quietly towards the bedroom door and looked through the crack to see the Corpse (red) naked and floating down the hallway towards her. She let out a scream and backed into a corner, shaking her head in disbelief. In the red-black room, she saw the Corpse (red) climb straight up a wall and across the ceiling, crashed down into the bed where they lay together, silent in each other's arms. Her sister kissed her upon the arm and she threw the Corpse (red) against the floor, saw the world turn upside-down at her red feet. The body rose up upon a bed of spinning mygg that sank back down into honeyed dreams, lost amidst all the Whore's (red) despair, a deep red river.

The Whore (red) remembered again the blue chequered harlequin who upon receiving the silver butterfly, led her into the white tent at the far side of the city. They ran through rancid streets, rats flooding from holes in walls bombed with calls for national freedom, ghosts lived in cages of imperialist bones, thin lakes of poverty. Finally, they reached a house atop the hill, the one she had heard through the perverse whispers of parlours, her husband scolding her in a room of fifty, her face filled with blood and shame. The Whore (red) had run through life and the infinity of others, the parallel suns of green and strange galaxies.

| A door opened. | There was a clean ordinary hallway and a silent man with a tattoo of a severed heart upon his |

right hand. The blue woman opened another door painted yellow, into a pale room. There was no one but a small boy with blonde hair sat upon a chair. Here they were now—entering the dungeon of all gossip. The master that grants a silver wish. She closed her eyes and held out her hand and there was a bottle stopped with a big cork. She ran into the street and rubbed her hair, her face, her breasts. She emptied the entire bottle onto her body and down around her sex, her glistening toes. The Whore (red) ran through the city and drank cognac, fucked three barley merchants in a tavern backroom, glancing from face to face as they kissed her and then one another, laughing at their callous folly. The men turned to watch her orgasm, a startled cherry appeared upon her lips, a morello witch ~~hovered~~. She was every river now.

Enchantment of Napoleon III

- *Verbena officinalis* (Verbena)
- *Vanilla planifolia* (Vanilla orchid)
- *Rosa hemisphaerica* (Sulphur rose)
- Droppings of a stork
- Green Chartreuse (liquor)
- *Schizophragma hydrangeoides* (Japanese hydrangea vine)

Friday, 2nd September, 1892

I painted my entire body blue, cobalt imported from smelted glass, the Norwegian Blaafarveværket rubbed across each ankle and between the toes. I scrawled a harlequin checkboard across the face and they named me the *Blå Jungfrun* after that wretched island covered in Easter witches. I had heard of children playing in the dirt, a stone pebble labyrinth eaten into the Baltic Sea. A beautiful widow alone in the tent tonight, wanton as giggling impresario led her into his mirrored cage and made all her sadness disappear, gulping schnapps as she watched thin shadows undress behind the linen screen. She kissed my blue hand and asked about Vaudevillian monsters, men that could twist and break an iron pipe on their throats. *Did magic really exist in Paris?* Upon the stage a man carried a dog that ran up and down his spine, leaping up to catch the trembling lamp. She showed me the lines of her hands and they matched her mouth. She spoke of a single thread of cotton sewn between the jawbone and ear—the face pulled in reverse like silver cobweb. I took the butterfly and we dashed into green night. The master was in his seventh body: a child but Perfect, a semi-angel. In his previous form as a Cathar, locked in an oubliette beneath a shameful yellow cross, he had been lifted higher on the most blinding of visions. The child was Saint Valentine on the hot and dusty Via Flaminia that saw all the way to Rimini, the sapphire blue sea. His blood was roses and strawberries, death everlasting. And now this glutton, bidden for immortality, threw krona and franc notes into his pale, sick hands.

The married woman in the city had spoken of cages of doves, of a vial of shining sperm. When she looked upon the fluid, she let out a little laugh—and asked again about the Mount of Venus, the fate line she had compared with her maidservant. I banished her into darkness with her trinket, an aphrodisiac the price of three stallions. The bourgeoisie will never learn, living ghosts wanting the touch of another but only frozen glass. I can hear the master praying in the next room. I have covered every mirror in the maison with black cloth. I lie in total darkness and need no other. I deny Rex Mundi—King of the World, the evil One. I dream only of my six other souls that wait in slumber, holding hands—all sisters.

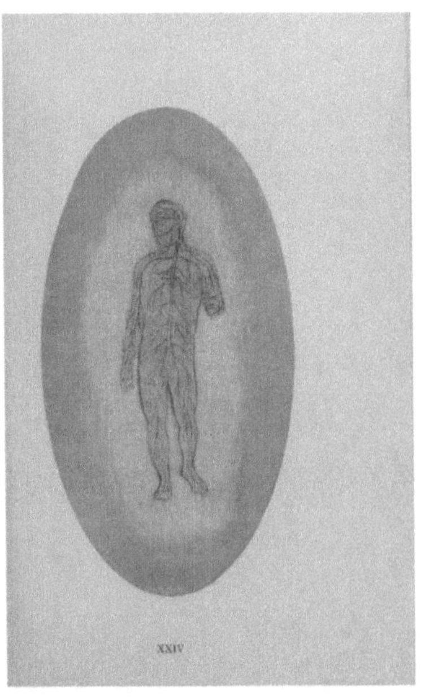

I am in charity, my children, with all the servants of God.

RED

RED

PHANTOM

RED

There were rose petals around the feet of the piano that formed a trial leading between the gas lamps, turned low around the dark oak bed. There was no sound through the mansion but from beyond, cries from the garden and across the lake, the weeping of wolves.

The Phantom (red) had been scared of dogs since she was bitten. A young girl running too close to the fences of the cattle farm in the village, yanked her hand back from the wire enclosing and looked deep into the guarding dog's eyes. It had switched—softened from vicious to suddenly very still and sad, its wet blue eyes looking down at the wound in the girl's forearm. It began to cry and she took her blood and smeared it across the wire fence before running home. Her grandmother bathed the girl in lavender beneath the new moon eaten whole by its own darkness, to make sure that she, only a child then, didn't become a wolverine at the end of January, feel her back surrounded with black hair and fangs.

The Phantom (red) had read books of faeries living in the lake, of Silverwhite the Knight murdering a sea troll emerging from the spray.

Her husband saw his likeness in the Storsjöodjuret on the cover of a book and threw them all into the kitchen furnace, hacked away into black smoke. His head was as small as a beechnut and crushed with sour light, dappled above the bowl of fish soup, jerked like a heron sat atop a rock as she began to undress. When they made love, she saw herself covered in grey egrets, their wings torn apart like angels flooding the blank ceiling.

On the first morning of their marriage, he had beckoned her into the chamber beneath the house—the silver key pressed deep into the wall. A hacksaw, a golden plate of lobes. This was his private world and atop the steel counter was the autopsy of a boy covered in the pox, his head broken open like a red melon, lungs hung in an ivory cage filled with canaries. As she looked into the child's crushed face, she saw only the same blue eyes of a dog breached apart.

On the first morning of their marriage, he had beckoned her into the chamber beneath the house—the silver key pressed deep into the wall. A hacksaw, a golden plate of lobes. This was his private world and atop the steel counter was the autopsy of a boy covered in the pox, his head broken open like a red melon, lungs hung in an ivory cage filled with canaries. As she looked into the child's crushed face, she saw only the same blue eyes of a dog breached apart.

When the Phantom (red) and the Corpse (red) left for Italy, the mountain sanatorium was filled with galleries of gasping men and women, all asleep behind panes of frosted glass and filled with rubber tubing, a wheezing engine behind the bed—their shadows risen as the nuns invoked a Catholic fool from beneath their azure cloaks. The nuns were cannibals and fed into the young, uncertain flesh of bodies more living, skin covered in yellow and scarlet fever, torsos running with custard beneath their dreadful appetites. When a man is starved, he will eat twice as much air, the handsome *mezzogiorno* machine that the nuns adored, strapped to his mouth and lung.

The Phantom (red) kept the Corpse (red) in a sealed room and passed bread, water and a beaker of red wine through the stone window. The air was clean and at night you could hear sparrows spiralling through the pink air.

The sheets were boiled in the basilica at the base of the mountain as the Phantom (red) locked the room to descend into a darkened valley. A woman filled with slow cholera, her bowels pumped out London water, the sweat of Camden rats—whispered in the sanatorium of a healer in the valley that could pluck out the seed of harm as if from a grape, of a man urinating purple bubonic, his youth returned like mother's kiss.

The Phantom (red) had followed the whispers of the dying into a villa at the end of the valley, green morning rising beyond the surrounding mountains. What did she hope? She saw her own sister led upon the autopsy table, the splitting of flesh, her husband's face leering into another cavity sprung white with poison. She had read too many books and believed she could reverse the evil sunset that crashed upon their twilit heads.

Whore (red)

She was revolted by the rusted little gate and the sprigs of rosemary hung upside-down along the doorway. There was no answer and inside she found a pair of dogs asleep at the fire almost dead now, the yellow flickering heat gliding her sadness through the stranger's house. The sound of music reminded her of childhood, of the Whore (red) playing across the garden, whilst she locked herself in the parlour and mother scolded her for being invisible, for feeding her arm to the dog.

The mansion was another abattoir and she saw the Corpse (red) led beneath a swinging pendulum like the butcher's hack. A voice calling from the enchanted kitchen, a man covered in silver hair and upon the table lay two Italian women, their bodies shining with oil. They rolled upon the floor and rubbed the golden vulva of the other, multiplying like cobwebs on fire. They placed little kisses upon the shoulders and thwacked huge mouthfuls of breast and buttock. Obscene shadows crawled across the stone floor below an orgy in the common villa. The Phantom (red) let out a dull cry and ran from the house with no secret, no whispered revelation, just the ordinary exchange of flesh for a bourgeois madman.

Her own body was like glass and she saw it in the evacuated faces frozen in the sanatorium, each peering across the Italian valley to face the blue sunrise. They coughed and cackled into linen bags hung from their rosaries. The smiling face of Agnes of Rome plastered in the floor, frescoes showing the miracle of a sealed tomb, the silent peach faces of the dead. A bell tower chiming into northern wind. She begged the cannibals to help, their mouths small and closed, eyes afraid to look into her huge pale fear. The Phantom (red) fled to the basilica again and the madman appeared, dressed in black finery and laughing into his watch.

The morning he visited the sanatorium, the nuns sinking into their mineral altars, ashamed in the presence of the well, his beautiful face. He was a hypnotist, famous and exiled from Switzerland, made an Austrian sleepwalk along a riverbed. The Phantom (red) shook as he hung the small watch in the face of the Corpse (red) and she looked into the numbers and saw her own extermination, the radius of enormousness speaking itself. The sanatorium leaped forward and every corpse yelled from its living throat—they passed from Italy into Constantinople, the purple chambers of Illyrian whores. The nuns wept at such a baffled spell. And then suddenly, the Corpse (red) spoke but with the voice of another. ~~She spoke of the colour red. Her head and arms twisted like a marionette. She was glowing and beautiful—glorious and young once more. She had always been the most beautiful sister.~~ She spoke of the colour red. Her head and arms twisted like a marionette. She was glowing and beautiful—glorious and young once more. She had always been the most beautiful sister.

And seeing her then, the Phantom (red) thought once more of Christmas morning when she had entered the bedroom to find the Corpse (red) and the Slave (red) covered in kisses, each sex alive and open. In dreams, she saw the touch of women as they held each other so close, much closer than a man could offer, for man was only the language of money and death. And here was her sister restored, a mirage floated atop the mountain.

They packed their things that morning and left on a train for Vienna, gulped in the air like new-borns. And as they left the shores of Denmark, the Phantom (red) saw the radiant eyeballs of a water spirit, a nøkken lived beneath the sea. The mansion was a castle through which the wolves howled and she laughed to kiss the face of the Whore (red)—a tree grown in the centre of the tower, its red keep covered in incest. She nestled inside the safety and protection of each and every room.

Doctor Gustav Szabo, Limmatquai, Zürich

Patient reference: 162ZB

Primary diagnoses: respiratory,

somnambulism

Location: Sanatorio di Santa Magdalene

Notes: The patient appeared distressed upon arrival and spoke in an accent I could not grasp well. She spoke of the colour red and the sister appeared frightened. I showed her my pocket watch after which the patient appeared more settled and spoke deeper and clearer. The sister became scared again and left the room. Upon which point I hung a piece of yellow topaz from a threaded hook and asked her to relax further. Her pupils dilated and pulse lowered significantly. I have included a short transcript for own personal notes.

Patient 162ZB: I am the colour red. The air is cold.

Szabo: Where are you now, can you tell me where you are at this very moment?

Patient 162ZB: The water is cold and we are waiting for news from home.

56

Szabo: The water is cold. Where is this water coming from?

Patient 162ZB: We drew a line. Merak through Dubhe. It was not hard to find our way north. And now we only dream in red.

Szabo: Where are you going?

Patient 162ZB: Towards the north. Can't you see?

(At this point, the patient lifted her right arm and extended her index finger towards the window.)

Szabo: Towards the sun?

Patient 162ZB: The sunsets are so red here. The sky is like a bathtub of blood. We lie in each other's arms in the cabin of the ship.

Szabo: Which ship are you aboard?

Patient 162BZ: We sleep together in our crimson nest and kiss the mouths and toes of each other. We live at the very edge of the world.

Szabo: You are very far from home.

(The patient begins to shake and assumes the arc-de-cercle, her body contorted off the bed. Her sister has returned to the door and looks distressed. Patient begins to shout.)

Patient 162BZ: Nova Zembla! Nova Zembla!

(Patient falls into a deep sleep.)

RED

RED

RED

SLAVE

A black tulip placed next to the golden frame—its calyx sealed shut with cool morning fear. A candle lit at dawn for the boats sinking beneath Malmö, rafts strapped with hazel and fly honeysuckle. A sapling grown from her own womb and placed in the ground beneath the mansion, a blue graveyard in the lake. ~~The Slave (red) felt her way through the corridors as though inside an aquarium, the voice of her mistress like a jellyfish, fluorescent and splattered upon the pillowcase.~~

The Slave (red) felt her way through the corridors as though inside an aquarium, the voice of her mistress like a jellyfish, fluorescent and splattered upon the pillowcase. In dreams, the Corpse (red) swelled twice in size and let out weeping howls as the brine spilled from its mouth and eyes, her poor hammerhead tears prayed to a crucifix stitched with Atlantic pearls, the grit of deepest rainstorms.

The Slave (red) was the mother of death and stood at the foot of the bed. The Corpse (red) had learned the red alphabet of the dead and over many nights had begun to sweat profusely, shouting words at the pane of glass, a single river of vowels flowered into the open mouth of the Phantom (red) that shook and denied—ran into a hallway to her own hated husband. His thin blonde face turned like an owl, barked about bloodletting, scrawled onto a yellow parchment to his twenty clerics. The walls, he felt, were obscene, and should be torn down, the mansion filling slowly with mewling cats that could smell the flesh beginning to curdle—a tumour grown inside the Corpse (red) like a new heart, an entirely new organ with its own soft voice, a song.

When the house was silent but for the howling wind, the Slave (red) approached the bed and placed her breast against the wall, saw a shadow drop from the golden frame. A gossamer of silk woven between the moon and bright waters of the lake. She walked through a door and onto the patio. It was past midnight and across the silver Eden, she saw ripples tremble as a tombstone emerged from the lake in white sprays of freshwater, the dead leaping like mackerel with rotten gills, a skull haloed in brightest rainbows. She waded into the cold without fear or anxiety. ~~The Slave (red) was the bravest of all because she had submitted to the greed of others and wanted none of it for herself.~~ The Slave (red) was the bravest of all because she had submitted to the greed of others and wanted none of it for herself.

All she wanted was risen now from the mud, a girl sank beneath the golden frame, danced atop the spiralling waves. A child given unto a chamber of the dead, lived in the red walls of the house that crashed and tore itself apart like a mad animal. It took its claws and dragged them down the shoulders of the Corpse (red), watching it arch—but suddenly calm like a blue orb, began to float up towards the ceiling.

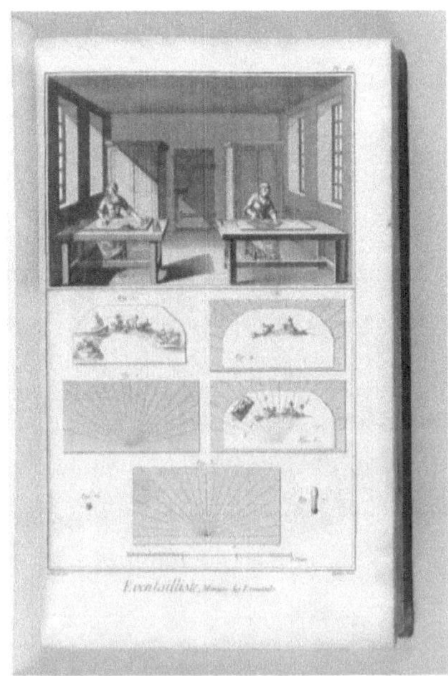

The Slave (red) had given birth to an orphan. On the second night, she took a handkerchief of money from beneath the floorboard and boarded a final boat, out towards the island shivering in white November fog. This was the worse month for a child to pass and it waited in the doctor's cellar, asleep in freezing ice. At the castle, the many rich looked upon the Slave (red) as though a plaything—laughed and taunted, until they saw the bloodshot in her eyes and a rope bound between her feet. They were led into a gigantic dining room, chandelier hung like grotesque cattle, the butchered insides of crystals. The bourgeoisie held hands in a constellation of their own sorrow and soon the illustrious seer arrived: a student of Swedenborg, face withered as a plum pit.

Every soul had come too close and nibbled on the ends of her earlobes, the broken ends of her fingertips.

The dead can swim through a human carcass as easily as breaststroke. And soon it took hold of her as the table began to creak and shake like a ship. The idiots started to laugh as though themselves cargo, jeering and sliding from side to side. Only the Slave (red) remained silent as the ancient woman produced a sheet of paper and began to write thin spindly words upon and spoke in a slow gentle voice, pronounced the name.

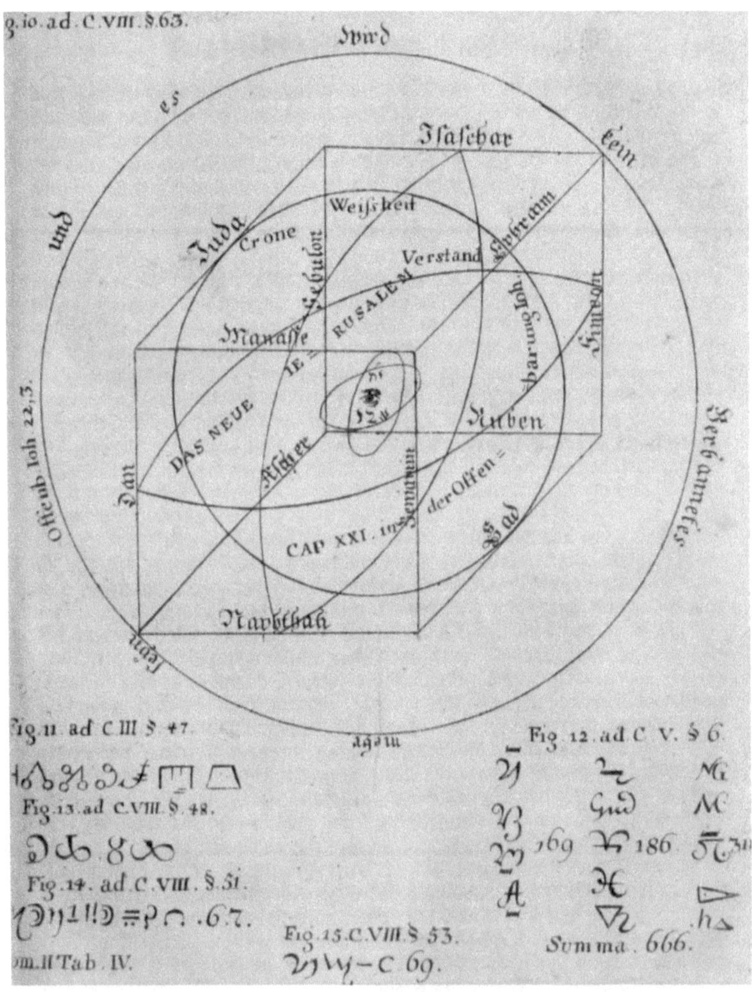

The Slave (red) let out a scream and leapt up, grabbed the parchment
to read inside dim candlelit. It made no sense, spoke of sadness for its

mother, all of them living inside the dream of a demon. She turned to face the crowd laughing harder now at her confusion and pain, the seer looking down, exhausted at the miserable theatre, ~~her hands caked in ruined gold.~~

Throwing the coins across the ... **the Slave (red)** ran from the house onto the ... beach, held the parchment until the boat returned and cast out again upon the water. Years sank into salt. But the words came back each night, and when **the Corpse (red)** fell ill she began to speak of the same walls like red wings, of the mansion becoming a room of blood. There were butterflies in hell, she said, far more beautiful than the one's on Earth. And angels that appear on their grotesque thorax. She spoke of **the Whore (red)** making love amongst flowers to whole battalions of soldiers in their summer-dazed garden, but there was no one there. She spoke of her glistening holes and showed them to **the Slave (red)** who held and was close with the speaker of the dead.

the Slave (red)

Throwing the coins across the table, **the Slave (red)** ran from the house onto an island beach, held the parchment until the boat returned and cast out again upon the water, tears sank into salt. But the words came back each night, and when **the Corpse (red)** fell ill she began to speak of the same walls like red wings, of the mansion becoming a cocoon of blood. There were butterflies in hell, she said, far more beautiful than the ones on Earth. And angels that appear on their grotesque thorax. She spoke of **the Whore (red)** making love amongst flowers to whole battalions of soldiers in their summer-dazed garden, but there was no one there! She spoke of her glistening holes and showed them to **the Slave (red)** who held and was close with the speaker of the dead.

When the Corpse (red) described a ghost returned from a lighthouse, the Phantom (red) shook its head and denied the screams of faeries tied to saplings, their hands and heads torn apart. The crucifix of the Lord, blue and aghast, witnessed the infested organs of the Corpse (red) begin to rise from her mouth and form a central machine inside the house, a mansion that ate splattered light along the purring insides of clocks. They held hands and began to waltz in small circles between the entrails of cows, the rubbery grey spleen swayed and stapled to their whalebone skirts. The blood pooled at their dappled feet and they made wishes to sperm whales, their mother sobbing on the night before Epiphany, her three daughters transformed into alchemists made of lead and silver.

On the day of her death, she saw a spider and all her hair turned white, colour of the moon.

It was winter again and the Slave (red) had heard the Corpse (red) speak of the same mirrored hallway as her dead orphan, a plateau of shining light where the snow littered her blonde head. When the Corpse (red) wheezed, the Phantom (red) heard it no longer as wind at the doorway nor the howling of a wolf. It was the beating of their hearts that fed blood through the walls, a transfusion from God through the skull of their sister exploding upon the bed. God broke her hip and then He broke her collarbone, and then drank away her skin like liquid cream until the silver skull rose from beneath the lake. A single kiss from the mouth of the Whore (red) and they span again into waltzing and passed along their dizzy hearts. The sisters exchanged each chamber of their own chests like red treasure, bracelets of capillaries snapped from the wrist of their withered Christ. And soon they were very quiet, and the Slave (red) began to weep, for she was the only one left alive. She was to feed the mansion with her own blood like an unborn child, to love and keep it close. Whether breathing or dead, she would cherish how much the Lord had given them, for their sickness was His and they snatched at His clothes and tore away His shame. They wanted the final robe that He held and covered His nakedness. It all belonged to them. Because His dream was theirs to devour.

Mother, mother… I am so far away… As are you… The walls of the house are bright red… Do not cry for me… I cry for you and all mortal souls… The world is but purgatory and each soul swims like a ship lost in fog… You live inside the dream of a demon… Beware mother, a gloved hand at the curtain… It dreams of all your sorrow… Death is but the brother of sleep and I weep to see you drown in its infernal mind… Its insatiable appetites… It craves the dreams of others… May you move from one room to the next and feel joy like the first day of spring… Winter melted… Flowers opening upon the sill… And I see you again, mother… Stood at the window, turned towards the sun risen above the lake… You close your eyes and meet the light… The warm silence of the sun… A child appearing in an empty room… It plays many tricks… And there is only red…. Look upon the mirror held in the right hand of Madame Ozanne and I shall be revealed once more… Look into the mirror… Mother… Can't you see… My hair is red… My bones are glass…

Images

1. Illustration from *Vier Bucher von Menslicher Proportion*, Albrecht Dürer (1528)

2. *The Alchemical Sisters*, Johann Daniel Mylius (1622)

3. *Dictionnaire Universel d'Histoire*, Charles Dessalines d'Orbigny (1849)

4. Detail from *The Adoration of the Magi*, Hieronymus Bosch (1475)

5. *The Book of Chess*, Jacobus de Cessolis (1483)

6. *Costume Design Sketches including a Bouffant Skirt, Hat, and Bodice*, Anonymous, French, 18th century (ca. 1785–90)

7. *The Rehearsal Onstage*, Edgar Degas (ca. 1874)

8. Book page image from *The Pedigree of the Devil*, Frederic T. Hall (1883)

9. Playing card (1700s)

10. *Death at the Ball*, Félicien Rops (1895)

11. *Dictionnaire Universel d'Histoire*, Charles Dessalines d'Orbigny (1849)

12. *Gloves* (ca. 1867)

13. *The Major Makes a Proposal (Inspecting a Bride in a Merchant's House)*, Pavel Fedotov (1848)

14. *Die Larven*, Albert Weisgerber (1907)

15. *Two women posed with a chair*, Albert Sands Southworth and Josiah Hawes (ca. 1850)

16. *Man Visible and Invisible*, Charles Webster Leadbeater (1902)

17. *Dictionnaire Universel d'Histoire*, Charles Dessalines d'Orbigny (1849)

18. Fresco by Francesco del Cossa and Cosme Tura (1470)

19. *Dancing Dragonflies*, Alfred Zimmermann (1903)

20. Book page image from *The Extravagant Shepherd, the Anti-Romance, or, The History of the Shepherd Lysis*, Charles Sorel (1654)

21. *Heures de Louis de Laval*, Jean Colombe (1480)

22. From the *First Love* cycle, Fritz Erler (1895)

23. Coat of arms of Friedrich Schiller (1759)

24. *Dictionnaire Universel d'Histoire*, Charles Dessalines d'Orbigny (1849)

25. Detail from *Repentant Magdalene*, Guido Cagnacci (1660s)

26. *The Sacrifice*, from *"The Satanic Ones"*, Félicien Rops (ca. 1882)

27. *Recueil de planches, sur les sciences, les arts libéraux, et les arts méchaniques: avec leur explication*, Denis Diderot (1762 72)

28. *Death and the Lansquenet*, Albrecht Dürer (1510)

29. *Opus Mago-Cabbalisticum et Theosophicum*, Georg von Welling (1735)

30. *Italian Landscape*, Camille Corot (ca. 1826–27)

31. *Theatre of Masks*, James Ensor (1908)

32. *The Dream of the Shepherd*, Ferdinand Hodler (1896)

Matthew Kinlin lives and writes in Glasgow. His two novels *Teenage Hallucination* (Orbis Tertius Press) and *Curse Red, Curse Blue, Curse Green* (Sweat Drenched Press) were released in 2021.